Cool Kid Friends Adventures In Las Vegas

The first children's workbook for Manish kids that are grown

Afi kingdom

Disclaimer

Cool kid has a series that incorporates art, paint, Rhythm rhyme arts and crafts all-in-one. Introducing the child to these things as well being self-sufficient and make learning fun instead of something to be neglected. It is not color base letting the reader use their imagination being able to create cool kid at one of his peers. Let's explore!

Forward by Jason Hampton:

Afi Kingdom is the most inspirational person you've never heard of not named Oprah, or roaming stages with a headset, screaming self-help jargon likes "manifest", or "massive action". It's because he's not trying to sell inspiration; he embodies it by being a living example.

I know Afi Kingdom as a Life Coach/Accountability Partner. Seeking to clarify my direction in growing a small business and merging my career interests with my love of travel, I got in touch with him. Three years later (with a worldwide pandemic interspersed), I have exceeded the progress I sought when I pursued Afi's help.

He didn't give me a 'golden ticket' piece of advice, or sell me some product. He simply connected. He listened. He asked me where I ultimately wanted to be. His ability to see multitudes of possibilities in the direst of situations helped me consider options I hadn't previously. Afi challenged me to discover what was within me to move toward my destiny. And I stayed inspired as I took personal action, but also saw via social media the steps he had taken to move toward his goals. When people say 'you need a new circle of friends', people like Afi Kingdom are the type of upgrade you need to make.

This book was thoughtfully written and illustrated by Afi Kingdom. It is the melding of many of his greatest attributes: educating others, helping others discovers the best of themselves, valuing learning, and living fully. Now this wisdom is being shared with future generations, coming from an educator of special resource children. As a result, Afi fully understands the science and art or learning and motivation. He has travelled the world extensively to incorporate the wealth of wisdom the world has to share on living full and purposeful lives.

This children's book is yet another way to share core worldviews widely known to improve satisfaction in one's self, their relationships with others, and life in general. Afi Kingdom champions literacy, obviously. More importantly, his valuation of the mind's power emphasizes the importance of critical thinking: that which leads to personal accountability, and ultimately personal freedom. Through a literary foundation we become more likely to gain exposure to truths and knowledge that lead us towards purposeful lives. From the knowledge we gain through learning, it becomes easier to embrace the individual nature of such purpose-filled life journeys. Afi Kingdom understands literacy aids in becoming less susceptible to developing a blind herd mentality.

Also central to this book's value is the worth of the word, and communication—what is said and not said can have equal importance. Two different messages can achieve the same influence, as one considers the applicable use of rhetoric to achieve a desired result. Historically writers and orators have been considered mythical figures because of their ability to impact people so profoundly. Afi

Kingdom's book encapsulates this magic when he engages adults and wide ranges of kids' ages in this book of few central themes: travel, lifelong learning, and mentorship.

The Romaire Bearden like collage artwork demonstrates the balance of imagination and practical groundedness Afi espouses. One gains the sense of travel's exhilaration, and the fun of learning about (and seeing) new places that have existed before us.

Afi Kingdom the lifelong artist highlights the importance of the visual arts in this book. He reminds us of its omnipresence in the history of civilizations, and its inextricable link to human history. The artist themselves understand the necessity of individualism, the propensity to innovate and synthesize influences. It's the process of how new movements and creations come into being. Even (and especially in) a digitalized age.

To indulge this book is to steep one's self in wonder, experience, curiosity, connection, love. Just as the central character benefits from the exposure he gains (through his mentor/mentee relationship), so will you and the child(ren) who gaze at these pages and cognitively process the magic mixture of wisdom, wonder, style, and education about to follow this page.

Enjoy. Many Times.

Jason Hampton

Table of Contents

Introduction

Cool kid is the kid who knows it all. The kids will hang with him get to know it all too. Cool kids friends are Jr the Hoop dreamer, little dude the one who isn't easily impressed. Pierre the Suave Debonair extraordinaire and Sarah the only girl in the crew who swears she knows more than the cool kid himself. In this adventure cool kid and Friends tour the city of Las Vegas. So no one cool kid don't be surprised if you pick up little facts throughout the tour as well as new words , places and concepts that I may not need now but will be important to me later.. Feel free to color and explore as you find out why your parents always talking about Las Vegas. Enjoy and have fun!

Prologue

Being an educator I noticed similarities and kids books. The similarity is they look like toys like they're made for kids. My style of education is a little different. I talk to kids and teach children the language that I want them to understand. I don't use baby words and things of that nature. I talked to the kids the way that even if they don't know what I mean they'll recognize the patterns and know how to respond. There are five main elements and purpose for this book.

Myself for example my mother read to me books that were for adults and older children. So I had a taste for books with no pictures at an early age. By 9 I was reading full live novels. The point is your kids will be with you expose them to. Of course they will have their own interest but it's okay to introduce them to new things and ideas. I will name off the five things to look out for in this book.

Cool kid is an older kid who is older than his friends. The point of cool kid is for kids to understand the importance of having a mentor. Having someone older and more experienced than them show them how to do cool things. The second thing is the importance of finding a tribe in people with common interest. All of cool kid's younger friends have their own characteristics and qualities that make them add value to their group. The third thing is exploration. Showing kids new food, places, travel, experiences, ethnicities Etc. Las Vegas is a place where you can experience a whole lot of things without going everywhere. This book will also show independence. This is the kind of book that as a child you will read and understand and also the fun facts will give you knowledge for your kid to be an All-Star like he is in college. Knowing not enough information isn't good. Is better to know more information.

Art as a major part of my life. I'm a writer; producer, director and I have a very creative mind. In this book I use pictures from my childhood that I actually made. I booked the structure when I was young. We have paint, cut and paste, in sketching. Sketching is a way to open up your mind to creative ideas. I feel like people should be experienced in all types of art and decide which one fits them the best.

Fourth thing about this book is to show kids Rhythm and Melody that will help them read. As a parent I would like for you to read the kids this book in Melody and teach them the fun fact. As the children Advance have them teach it back to you and show you what they've learned through repetition and persistence. The last thing about this book is the plant seeds for kids to embrace traveling and exploration. Exploration builds character and everyone should aspire to have that. Even the Manish grown up children like I was lol. Enjoy cool kid and Friends Adventure to Las Vegas. This will be one of many. Even if you were an adult you may learn something about Las Vegas as well that you didn't know before. Let's dive in and take a trip

Welcome

To

Las Vegas!

Las Vegas was created in

1911.

Out of Every Place in the

World,

It's the Gambling Heaven!

Fun Facts

The Las Vegas Strip is 4.2 miles long. 15 of the largest luxury hotels are located on the Las Vegas Strip. The Las Vegas sign was made in 1959. Although the Las Vegas Strip actually is, Las Vegas County itself is still located in Clark County.

People fly around the

world to hit the Jackpot,

Wishing you the best of

luck if your game is craps,

cards or the slots!!

Fun Fact

Las Vegas has been the core of the gambling world since the 1960s. Although Vegas aren't the only place to gamble it holds the most casinos and places to gamble and bet on fights etc. This makes it the most lucrative destination.

If you love food,

Vegas, is the place to be!

With so much variety,

You will faint when you

see!!

Fun Fact

Las Vegas is famous for its variety of food and comparative pricing. The word buffet was used to replace the term Smorgasbord because of his variety of food and being self served. The (all-you-can-eat) style Buffet as we know it was introduced in 1956 by Mr. MacDonald.

Families come to Vegas, to

see the live shows.

With Performers and

Celebrities that everyone

knows!

Fun Fact

Vegas are the place for Grand entertainment. Popular acts such as Britney Spears, Cher, and Barbra Streisand perform live shows their regular year-round. As for the past Liberace and Elvis were very popular. They're also exclusive acts such as Blue Man Group classic showcases comedy magic Etc.

whatever you're vice is Vegas have it to

offer

If you love heights, there is the Stratosphere Tower!

You'll be on top of the world with all of the Power!!!

Fun Fact

The stratosphere is the tallest free-standing observation tower in the US, and it's the third tallest structure behind the Sears Tower in the newly-developed CN Tower in Toronto. It is a part of the hotel casino as well and at one point had a roller coaster at top of it. There you will also find a top of the world revolving restaurant.

Circus Circus is a family destination.

With all the games and rides it will keep your

Heart racing!

Fun Fact

Circus Circus at the largest Big Top circus in the entire world. It opened in 1968. In Columbus lions with Circus Circus, to accommodate teens and adults The Adventure Dome was built which is an amusement park also produced in 1993.

Visiting Caesars Palace is

like traveling to Rome for a

day.

Afterwards, you can flee to

Excalibur for a Medieval

Stay!

Fun Fact

Caesar's Palace was established in 1966 to give guests an experience of what it would be like to live in the Roman Empire. Excalibur was built in 1992 with the medieval times and has a castle theme. Its name comes from the famous King Arthur's sword named Excalibur.

Shoot to the "Top of the

Eiffel Tower" in Paris, for

a spectacular scene of the

city.

Or you may zoom through

New York, New York on a

roller coaster,

Maybe, even spot the

Statue of Liberty!

Fun Fact

The Paris hotel opened in 1999 and has a replica of the Eiffel Tower inside going up through the hotel. You can elevator up for a scenic view or dine at the Eiffel Tower restaurant. New York New York was made in 1997 and has a replica of skyscrapers as well as the Statue of Liberty. Also there is a roller coaster that rides through it for an unforgettable experience.

You can ride in a

helicopter; even see the

Hoover Dam,

The Big kids can hit the

range when you get back

to the land.

Fun Fact

The Hoover Dam is located in the desert between Nevada and Arizona. It is a tourist destination with millions of people coming every year. The helicopter tour is one of the favorites looking over the desert and all of Las Vegas Skyline. The gun store is a range that was popular because it is one of the only places you can access semi-automatic weapons without a license.

T.V's in the mirrors, hot tubs in the floor,

Vegas have luxury and you will be back for more and more!

Fun Fact

____Las Vegas has the most luxurious Hotel suites in the world! If you want a tiger and a hot tub Vegas can get you that. Whatever your imagination is you will get your fix. You can get the most state-of-the-art amenities, architecture, and spectacular views!

If the clubs and dancing is

your scene, get

Dressed, Bust a Move,

and Do YOUR

THING!

Fun Fact

Out of the most profitable hotels in the world, Vegas hold 1/4 of those. That is because they have the most lavish and exotic clubs able to accommodate anything. It is also very popular with celebrities and you can spot them year round!

Boxing and U.F.C,

yes Vegas is the place!

Watch gladiators combat,

and even change

Their face!

Fun Fact

Las Vegas at the home of the prize fighter. It is the most lucrative place to win money but it's also the best place to lose. It is not the only place where the fights are held, but Main Event Marquee matchups are almost exclusively held there. Hotels and flight prices fluctuate increasingly because of the visitors coming in the day

or on the weekend.

Vegas are the best for high end shopping!

Get your cash and credit card, go get your Gear poppin!

Fun Fact

Las Vegas is the main attraction like New York, for its high-end retail options. Louis Vuitton, Gucci, Fendi, is all there in one place at the Fashion Show Mall. There are also plenty of bargains in Vegas for those who don't want to spend a lot of money and get more bangs for their buck.

When people put your
love under a microscope.

Skip planning, take a ride,
and go elope!

Fun Fact

Las Vegas is the marriage capital of the world. Partially because you can gets a marriage license within minutes skipping the usual process. People who want to avoid the extravaganza or typical wedding and just want to make it legal can go through a drive-thru wedding. Pretty cool right? Can you imagine being married without leaving your car? That experience will be convenient as well as memorable. Just another perk in Vegas!

So all and all Vegas is the place to be!

So take a plane, ride the train, and you soon

You will see!!!!

Epilogue

I hope you the parent as well as the child enjoyed this book. I hope that you learned some new things about Vegas. I also hope that you are inspired to try new things. When you get old enough to go to Vegas or just in life in general. Have an open mind, try new excursions and learn yourself. That way you can be the best possible version of you. Revisit this book when you're a little older and pass it down to those that come after you. Teach them through this book The Power of learning, independence, travel and exploring, having a mentor, being creative and opening up your mind to new things. See you on the next adventure with Cool Kid and Friends.

Practice What You Learned Quiz

1. How long is the Las Vegas Strip?

....

....

....

2. True or false is Las Vegas the most lucrative destination?

....

....

....

3. What is a show in Las Vegas that you would like to see?

....

....

....

4. What is the tallest free-standing observation tower in the U.S?

....

....

....

5. Which fun place was built first the Adventuredome or Circus Circus?

....

....

....

6.What is Excalibur and where did the name come from?

....

....

....

7. What are two hotels in Las Vegas that are named after famous places?

....

....

....

8. What is the best way to see and experience all of Vegas in the air?

....

....

....

....

9. Look through Google images and search mansions in Vegas. Point which one you like in aspire to get Cut it out and save it. Ask your parents to put on the refrigerator for you to save!

....

....

....

....

....

10. How often do people go to visit Vegas?

....

....

....

11. Is Vegas the most popular place for Price fighting?

....

....

....

....

12. True or False Vegas has things for you to do if you have a lot of money or even if you have a little bit of money?

....

....

....

13. True or False can people get married in Vegas in the Drive-Thru?

....

....

....

14. What is your favorite thing you learned about Las Vegas?

....

....

....

15. What activities interested you? What is the first thing you would do if you were to travel to Vegas with your family or frierds?

....

....

....

16. I will make sure to reread this book and share with others because I have learned attributes, skills AND HAVE A CREATIVE MINDSET ! I look forward to being creative , exploring and becoming independent. I can't wait to share what I have learned with the people who I love.

....

....

....

.........Then End......

Made in the USA
Columbia, SC
15 December 2024